to Anna & Victoria,

Happy Christmas,

love

Mhairi &

Naomi
xxx

FIVE MINUTE
Sleepy Time Tales

FIVE MINUTE
Sleepy Time Tales

Written by
Derek Hall, Alison Morris
and Louisa Somerville

SIENA

Illustrated by
Natalie Bould, Lynn Breeze, Maureen Galvani, Mary Hall,
Virginia Margerison, Paula Martyr, Julia Oliver, Martin Orme, Gillian Toft,
Charlie Anne Turner, Kerry Vaughan, Jenny Williams, Kirsty Wilson

Designed by Louise Millar

This is a Siena Book
Siena is an imprint of PARRAGON

PARRAGON
Queen Street House
4 Queen Street
Bath BA1 1HE, U.K.

Copyright © 1998 PARRAGON

Created and produced for Parragon by
Linda Watters Book Packaging
8 Trent Close, Shenley
Herts WD7 9HX, UK

ISBN 0-75252-772-X

Printed in Singapore

Contents

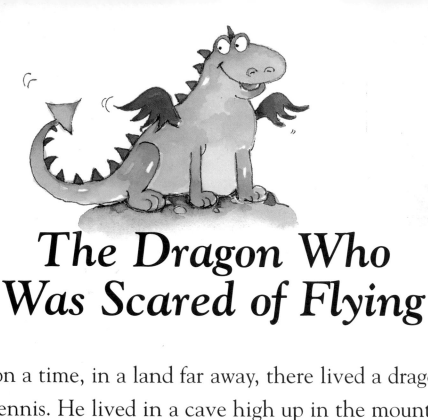

The Dragon Who Was Scared of Flying

Once upon a time, in a land far away, there lived a dragon named Dennis. He lived in a cave high up in the mountains. All his friends lived in caves nearby, and his own brothers and sisters lived right next door. Now you would think that Dennis would have been a very happy dragon, surrounded by his friends and family, wouldn't you? Well, I'm sorry to say that Dennis was, in fact, a very unhappy and lonely dragon.

The reason for this was that Dennis was scared of flying. Every day his friends would set off to have adventures, leaving poor Dennis behind on his own. Dennis would stare out of his cave at the departing dragons. How he wished he could join them!

6

After they had gone, he would stand on the ledge outside his cave, trying to build up the courage to fly. But as soon as he looked over the edge, he felt all giddy and had to step back. Then he would crawl back into his cave defeated and spend the rest of the day counting stalagtites on the ceiling or rearranging his collection of bat bones.

Every evening, the other dragons would return with amazing tales of what they had been up to that day. "I rescued a damsel in distress," one would say.

"I fought the wicked one-eyed giant and won," boasted another.

"I helped light the fire for a witch's cauldron," announced a third.

"What have you been up to?" Dennis's sister Doreen used to ask him.

"Oh... um... this and that," Dennis would reply mournfully, looking down at his scaly toes. Then Doreen would lead him out of the cave and try to teach him to fly. Dennis would take a running jump and flap his wings furiously but his feet would stay firmly on the ground. Then the other dragons would laugh so much that, in the end, he always gave up.

One day, Dennis could stand it no longer. The other dragons flew off as usual to find adventure but Dennis, instead of retreating into his cave, set off down the mountain side. It was very tiring having to walk. Dennis had never really been further than from his cave to the ledge and back, and soon he was puffing and panting. He was about to rest at the side of the path when his eye was caught by something colourful in the distance. Down in the valley he could make out some brightly coloured tents, and now he could hear the faint strains of music drifting up to him. "I'd better take a closer look," thought Dennis. "Maybe I can have an adventure, like the other dragons!" He got so excited at the thought of his very own adventure that he started to run. Then he got all out of breath and had to stop altogether for a while.

At last Dennis reached the tents and found himself in a world more exotic than he could ever have imagined. He was surrounded by strange, four-legged creatures, such as he had never seen before. There was a yellow creature that roared and another one with stripes and fierce teeth. There were also quite a few hairy creatures with long tails. These ones were dressed up to look like boys and girls. Can you guess what all these creatures were? Of course, Dennis had never seen a lion or a tiger or a chimpanzee before. He thought they were very peculiar! The animals thought Dennis was very odd, too. They stood in a circle around him. "How strange," snarled the lion. "A slimy thing with wings!"

"It doesn't look very fit!" growled the tiger, flexing his claws.

"Look at its funny, knobbly tail," giggled the chimpanzees.

Dennis began to feel unhappy and unwanted again, but at that moment he heard a friendly voice saying, "Hello, there! Welcome to Chippy's Circus. I'm Claude the clown. How do you do?"

Dennis turned round. Now he felt really confused, for standing behind him was a man with the unhappiest face Dennis had ever seen. He had great sad eyes and a mouth that was turned down so far that it seemed to touch his chin. Yet he spoke so cheerfully!

"I'm Dennis the dragon," said Dennis.

"A dragon, eh?" said Claude. "Well, we've never had a dragon in the circus before. Might be quite a crowd puller! Would you like to join the circus?" he asked.

"Oh, yes please," cried Dennis.

"Very well," said Claude. "I'm sure you're very talented," he added.

So Dennis joined the circus and was happy for the first time in his life. The other animals became quite friendly now that they knew what he was. Claude taught Dennis to ride the unicycle and to do acrobatic tricks. He also learned how to dive into a bucket of water. He didn't mind that a bit because his slimy skin was quite waterproof! Now, as you know, dragons are particularly

10

good at breathing fire, so Dennis soon became the circus's champion fire-eater. Folk would come from far and near to see Dennis shooting flames high into the dark roof of the big top.

One evening Dennis had just finished his fire-eating act. He was eating an icecream to cool his hot throat and watching Carlotta, the tight-rope walker. She was pirouetting high up on the rope as usual. Then all at once she lost her footing and Dennis saw to his horror that she was going to fall. He dropped his icecream and, without thinking, flapped his wings furiously. As Carlotta fell, Dennis found himself flying up towards her. He caught her gently on his back and flew down to the ground with her clinging on tightly. The crowd roared and burst into applause. They obviously thought it was all part of the act.

"Thank you, Dennis," whispered Carlotta in Dennis's ear. "You saved my life."

Dennis was overjoyed. Not only had he saved Carlotta's life, he had also learned to fly. And he said with a grin, "I do declare that flying is actually rather fun."

The Toys That Ran Away

"Put your toys away, Lucy," said Lucy's mother from the kitchen, "it's time to get ready for bed."

Lucy gave a great big sigh. "Do I really have to?" she asked, knowing full well what the answer was going to be.

"Yes, of course you do," said her mother. "You shouldn't have to be told each time to put your toys away. You really don't look after them properly."

It was true. Lucy never had been very good at looking after her toys. Once she left her beautiful new doll outside in her pram and she had become ruined after it rained. Then she had carelessly dropped her tea set on the floor and some of the cups had broken. And she was forever just pushing all her toys back in the cupboard in a hurry, instead of putting them away carefully. Worse still, when she was in a temper, she would throw her toys, and sometimes she would even kick them.

Tonight Lucy was in another of her 'can't be bothered' moods. She grabbed a handful of toys and threw them into the cupboard. In first went some dolls, which all landed on their heads and then fell in a heap. Next Lucy threw in the little tables and chairs from the doll's house. They landed with a bounce and came to a stop in the corner. Without even looking behind her, Lucy then picked up some puzzles and a skipping rope, and tossed them into the cupboard, too. They landed with a crash on the floor of the cupboard as well.

"That's that," said Lucy. She closed the cupboard door, squashing the toys even more, and went into the bathroom to have her bath.

Inside the toy cupboard Teddy, one of the toys, spoke. "I'm not going to stay here a moment longer," he said.

"Nor me," said Katie the ragdoll.

13

"If we aren't going to be loved, we aren't staying either," chimed the doll's house furniture.

"I want to be somewhere where I'm not thrown around," said one of the puzzles.

"So do we," said the roller blades.

One after another, all the toys agreed that they weren't going to stay. They decided they would all go back to Toyland and wait to be given to some children who would love them more.

The next morning, Lucy decided that she would play with her skipping rope. When she opened the toy cupboard, she couldn't believe her eyes. All the toys had vanished. The shelves were completely empty.

At first Lucy thought her mother had moved them, but her mother said she hadn't. "I expect you've put them somewhere yourself, Lucy, and can't remember where you've left them," said her mother, not very helpfully. All day, Lucy searched high and low for her missing toys, but they were nowhere to be found. She went to bed in tears that night, wondering if she would ever be able to play with her toys again. She was already missing them terribly.

That night, Lucy was suddenly woken by a noise in her bedroom. Was she seeing things or was that a little fairy at the bottom of her bed? "Who are you?" asked Lucy.

"I am the special messenger from Toyland," replied the fairy. "I have been sent to tell you that all your toys have run away back to Toyland, because you treated them badly."

"Oh, I do miss my toys so much," cried Lucy.

"Well, if you really do, then you had better come and tell them yourself," said the fairy.

With that, the fairy floated over to Lucy and took her hand. The fairy then beat her wings so fast that they became a blur. At the same time Lucy felt herself being lifted from her bed. Out of Lucy's bedroom window they both flew, across fields and forests, until it became too misty for Lucy to see anything at all.

Suddenly, they were floating down to the ground. The mist lifted, and Lucy found herself in the grounds of a huge fairy-tale castle with tall, pointed turrets and warm, yellow lights twinkling from the windows.

"This is Toyland Castle," exclaimed the fairy, as she led Lucy to a large red door.

The fairy knocked on the door. "Do enter, please," said a voice.

Lucy found herself in a large, cosy room with a huge log fire. Sitting in the corner was a kindly looking little man wearing a carpenter's apron and holding a broken wooden doll. "Hello," he said, "you've come to ask your toys to return, haven't you?"

"Well... er... yes," said Lucy, not really quite knowing what to say.

"It's up to them to decide, of course," said the little man. "They only come back here if they are mistreated. If they are broken, I repair them, and then they go to other children who love them more."

"But I *do* love my toys," wept Lucy.

"Then come and tell them yourself," smiled the little man.

He led Lucy into another room, and there, to her surprise, were all her toys. Not only that, but they were all shiny and new again. Nothing was broken or chipped or scratched.

Lucy ran up to her toys. "Please, toys, please come home again. I really do love you and miss you, and I promise I shall never mistreat you again," she cried. She picked up Teddy and gave him a big hug. Then she did the same thing to all the other toys.

"Well, it's up to the toys now," said the little man. "You must go back home again with the fairy messenger and hope that they will give you another chance."

With that, the fairy messenger took Lucy's hand, and soon they were floating over her own garden again and through her bedroom window. Lucy was so tired she didn't even remember falling asleep when she got into bed.

In the morning she awoke, still rather sleepy, and rushed to the toy cupboard. There, neatly lined up on the shelves, were all her toys. Lucy was overjoyed. From that day on, she always treated her toys well and took great care of them.

Lucy never was quite sure whether the whole thing was a dream or not, but it certainly did the trick whatever it was. There was one thing that really puzzled her though. If it had just been a dream, why were all the toys so shiny and new again?

Mr Mole Gets Lost

Mr Mole poked his little black nose out from the top of one of his mole hills and gave a great big sniff of the air. Then he sniffed again. And then a third time just to make sure. "Oh dear," he thought, "it smells like it's going to rain."

Mr Mole didn't like the rain one bit. Every time he got caught in the rain his plush little velvet fur coat got all wet and drippy, and he left muddy footprints all over his underground burrow. But worse still, the rain got in through the holes in his mole hills and then everything got all soggy and took days to dry out.

Well, the skies got darker and darker, and very soon little spots of rain began to fall. Then the spots became bigger. And then bigger still. Before long, all you could see before your eyes were big, straight rods of rain bouncing off the leaves on the trees, pounding the ground and turning everything muddy and wet.

Mr Mole had never seen rain like it. He sat in his burrow in the middle of the meadow wishing it would stop. But it just kept raining and raining. Soon the rain started entering his burrow. First it went drip, drip, drip through the holes in his mole hills, and then it became a little river of water in the bottom of his burrow. Then the little river became a bigger, faster-flowing river and suddenly Mr Mole was being washed along by it. Through the tunnels of his burrow he went, this way and then that, as the water gushed and poured through his underground home.

The next thing he knew he was being washed out of his burrow completely as the rain water carried him off down the meadow. Down he went, not knowing which way up he was or where he was going. Now he was being washed through the woods at the bottom of the meadow, but still the water carried him on, bouncing and turning him until he was dizzy and gasping for breath.

Suddenly, he came to a halt. The rain water gurgled and trickled around him and then flowed onwards, as he found himself stuck firmly in the branches of a bush. "Oh dear," Mr Mole said as he got himself free. "Goodness me, where can I be?" he thought. Mr Mole looked around him, but being a very short-sighted mole – as most moles are – he couldn't make out any of the places that were familiar to him. Worse still, he couldn't smell any smells that were familiar to him. He was completely lost, far from home, and had no idea how to get back again. Now, to make things worse, it was starting to get dark.

"Woo-oo-oo-oo-oo!" said a voice suddenly. Mr Mole nearly jumped out of his moleskin with fright. "I wouldn't stay here if I were you," said the voice again. Mr Mole looked up and found himself face to face with an enormous owl. "Don't you know it's not safe in the woods at night?" asked the owl. "There are snakes and foxes and weasels and all sorts of nasty creatures that you really wouldn't like to meet."

"Oh dear!" was all Mr Mole could think of saying. He told the owl of his terrible watery journey and how he was lost and didn't know how to get back home again.

"You need to talk to Polly Pigeon," said the owl. "She is a homing pigeon and she lives near your meadow. She can show you the way home. But we'll have to find her first. Stay close to me, mind, and look out for those snakes, foxes and weasels I told you about."

Mr Mole didn't need telling twice. He stayed so close to the kindly owl that every time the owl stopped or turned round to talk to Mr Mole, Mr Mole bumped right into him!

Through the dark, dangerous woods they went. Every now and again, there would be an unfriendly noise, such as a deep growl or a hiss, coming from the dense, tangled trees, but Mr Mole didn't want to think about that too much, so he just made sure that he never lost sight of the owl.

Finally, just when Mr Mole thought that he couldn't go a step further, they came to a halt by an old elm tree.

"Hallo-oooo," called the owl.

They were in luck. Polly Pigeon was waking up, and they found her just in time for she was about to continue her journey home.

"Please," said Mr Mole, "I'm afraid I'm terribly lost and don't know how to get back to my meadow. Will you take me there?"

"Of course I will," said Polly Pigeon. "We'd better let you rest here a while first, though. But we must go before it gets light."

So Mr Mole was soon trudging wearily back to his meadow, following as closely behind Polly Pigeon as he was able. Just as the first rays of sun lit the morning sky, Mr Mole smelled a very familiar smell. It was his meadow! He was almost home!

Soon, he was back in his own burrow. It was so wet and muddy, however, that the first thing he did was build some new tunnels higher up the meadow so that the rain wouldn't wash down into them so easily. Then he settled down to eat one of his supplies of worms, and fell into a deep, well-earned slumber.

The Red Daffodil

It was spring time and all the daffodils were pushing their heads up towards the warmth of the sun. Slowly, their golden petals unfolded to let their yellow trumpets dance in the breeze. One particular field of daffodils was a blaze of gold like all the others – but right in the middle was a single splash of red. For there in the middle was a red daffodil.

From the moment she opened her petals, the red daffodil knew she was different from the other flowers. They sneered at her and whispered to each other. "What a strange, poor creature!" said one.

"She must envy our beautiful golden colour," said another.

24

And indeed it was true. The red daffodil wished very much that she was like the others. Instead of being proud of her red petals, she was ashamed and hung her head low. "What's wrong with me?" she thought. "Why aren't there any other red daffodils in the field?"

Passers-by stopped to admire the field of beautiful daffodils. "What a wonderful sight!" they exclaimed. And the daffodils' heads swelled with pride and danced in the breeze all the more merrily.

Then someone spotted the red daffodil right in the middle of the field. "Look at that extraordinary flower!" the man shouted. Everyone peered into the centre of the field.

"You're right," said someone else, "there's a red daffodil in the middle." Soon a large crowd had gathered, all pointing and laughing at the red daffodil.

She could feel herself blushing even redder at the attention. "How I wish my petals would close up again," she said to herself in anguish. But try as she might, her fine red trumpet stood out for all to see.

Now, in the crowd of people gathered at the edge of the field was a little girl. People were pushing and shoving and she couldn't see anything at all. At last, her father lifted her high upon his shoulders so that she could see into the field. "Oh!" exclaimed the little girl in a very big voice. "So that's the red daffodil. I think it's really beautiful. What a lucky daffodil to be so different."

And do you know, other people heard what the little girl said and they began to whisper to each other, "Well, I must say, I actually thought myself it was rather pretty, you know." Before long, people were praising the daffodil's beauty and saying it must be a very special flower. The red daffodil heard what the crowd was saying. Now she was blushing with pride and held her head as high as all the other daffodils in the field.

The other daffodils were furious. "What a foolish crowd," said one indignantly. "We are the beautiful ones!" They turned their heads away from the red daffodil and ignored her. She began to feel unhappy again.

By now word had spread far and wide about the amazing red daffodil and people came from all over the land to see her. Soon, the king's daughter got to hear about the red daffodil. "I must see this for myself," said the princess. She set off with her servant and eventually they came to the field where the red daffodil grew. When the princess saw her, she clapped her hands with glee.

"The red daffodil is more beautiful than I ever imagined," she cried. Then she had an idea. "Please bring my pet dove," she said to her servant. The man looked rather puzzled, but soon he returned with the bird. "As you know," said the princess to the servant, "I am to be married tomorrow and I would dearly love to have that red daffodil in my wedding bouquet."

The princess sent the dove into the middle of the field and it gently picked up the daffodil in its beak and brought her back to where the princess stood. The princess carried the daffodil back to the palace. She put the daffodil in a vase of water and there she stayed until the next day.

In the morning, the princess's servant took the red daffodil to the church. She could hear the bells and see all the guests assembling for the wedding ceremony. Then she saw the princess arrive in a coach driven by four white horses. How lovely the princess looked in her white gown and her head crowned with deep red roses.

As the servant reached the church door, the princess's lady-in-waiting stepped forward holding a huge bouquet of flowers into which she placed the red daffodil just as the flowers were handed to the princess. For a while, the red daffodil was overcome by the powerful scents of the other flowers in the bouquet, but when at last she looked around her she realised, with astonishment, that all of them were red. There were red daisies, red lilies, red carnations and red foxgloves. "Welcome," said one of the daisies, "you're one of us." And for the first time in her life, the red daffodil felt really at home.

After the wedding, the princess scattered the flowers from her bouquet among the flowers in her garden. Every spring, when she opened her petals, the red daffodil found she was surrounded by lots of other red flowers, and she lived happily in the garden for many, many years.

The Mean King and the Crafty Lad

There was once a king who was as mean as he was rich. He lived in a great palace where he spent his days counting his bags of gold coins. Meanwhile his subjects lived in great poverty. Sometimes the king would summon his page to prepare the royal carriage. Then the king would set forth in his great, golden coach to survey his kingdom.

Now not only was the king extremely rich, but he was very vain. As he passed his subjects working in the field, he liked them to bow to him and pay him compliments. "How handsome you look today, your majesty!" they would call, or "How well the colour pink suits you, Sire!"

His head would swell with pride as he moved on. "My people truly adore me!" he would say.

But for all their complimentary words, the people hated their king. They resented the fact that the king lived in splendour while his subjects toiled hard all their lives. At last a secret meeting was called among the peasants. "Let's sign a petition demanding our rights!" cried one man.

"And fair pay!" shouted another. They all cheered and clapped their hands.

"Who's going to write down our demands?" called an old woman. Now the crowd was hushed, for none of them knew how to read or write.

"I know what we can do instead," called a voice from the back. Everyone turned round to see a young lad in rags. "Let's march on the palace!" he cried.

"Yes!" roared the crowd.

As the angry mob reached the palace, the king saw them and sent out his guard dogs. The peasants were forced to flee for their lives with the dogs snapping at their ankles. Not until the last peasant was out of sight did the king call off his dogs.

"Good work!" he cried.

From then on, however, life became even harder for the people because the king was on his guard in case they marched on the castle again. Now, when he went out and about in his kingdom, he was always accompanied by his hounds.

Eventually, another secret meeting was called. "What can we do?" the people said. "We will never be able to get past those savage dogs."

"I've got an idea," came a familiar voice. It was the ragged lad again. For a while there was uproar as folk accused him of having nearly lost them their lives. "Please trust me," pleaded the lad. "I know I let you down, but this time I've got a well thought-out plan to get the king to give up his money." In the end, the peasants listened to the boy's scheme and decided to let him try.

The next day, the boy hid in a branch of a tree that overhung the palace garden. With him he had some dog biscuits, in which he had hidden a powerful sleeping pill. He threw the biscuits on to the palace lawn and waited. Some time later, as the boy had hoped, the king's hounds came out on to the lawn. They headed straight for the biscuits and gobbled them up. Soon they were fast asleep, one and all.

Quickly the lad slid out of the tree and, donning a large black cape, he ran round to the front of the palace and rapped on the door. A sentry opened the door. "Good day," said the lad, "I am Victor, the world-famous vet. Do you have any animals requiring medical attention?"

"No," replied the sentry, slamming the door in the lad's face. Just then voices could be heard from within the palace. After a few moments, the sentry opened the door again and said, "As a matter of fact, we do have a bit of a problem. Step inside."

The sentry led the lad out to the lawn where the king was weeping over the dogs' bodies. "Oh, please help," he cried. "I need my dogs. Without them I may be besieged by my own people."

The lad pretended to examine the dogs. He said to the king, "I have only seen one case like this before. The only cure is to feed the animals liquid gold."

"Liquid gold?" exclaimed the king. "Wherever shall I find liquid gold?"

"Fear not," said the lad, "I have a friend – a witch – who lives in the mountains. She can turn gold coins into liquid gold. You must let me take the dogs – and a bag of gold – to her and she will cure them."

Well, the king was so beside himself with fear that he readily agreed. The sleeping dogs were loaded on to a horse-drawn cart, and the king gave the lad a bag of gold saying, "Hurry back, my dogs are most precious."

Off went the lad, back to his home. His mother and father helped him unload the dogs, who by now were beginning to wake up. They took great care of the dogs, who were glad to be looked after kindly for once. The next day the lad put on the cloak again and returned to the palace. "The good news is," he said to the king, "that the cure is working. The bad news is that there was only enough gold to revive one dog. I'll need all the gold you've got to cure the others."

"Take it all," screamed the king, "only I must have my dogs back tomorrow!" He opened the safe and threw his entire stock of gold on to another cart, which the young lad dragged away.

That night the lad gave each of the king's subjects a bag of gold. The next morning he led the dogs back to the palace. To his surprise, the king didn't want them back. "Now I have no gold," he said, "I don't need guard dogs."

Then the lad saw that the king had learned his lesson, and he told the king what had really happened. And to everyone's joy, the king said the peasants could keep their bags of gold. As for the king, he kept the dogs as pets and became a much nicer person.

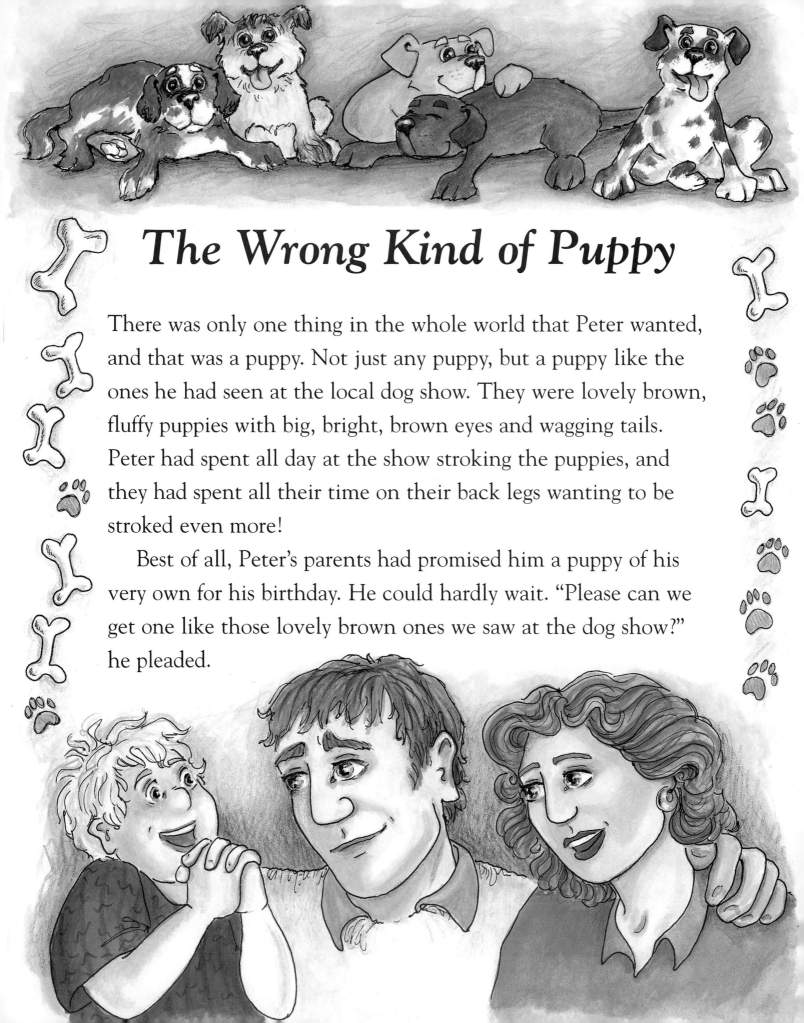

The Wrong Kind of Puppy

There was only one thing in the whole world that Peter wanted, and that was a puppy. Not just any puppy, but a puppy like the ones he had seen at the local dog show. They were lovely brown, fluffy puppies with big, bright, brown eyes and wagging tails. Peter had spent all day at the show stroking the puppies, and they had spent all their time on their back legs wanting to be stroked even more!

Best of all, Peter's parents had promised him a puppy of his very own for his birthday. He could hardly wait. "Please can we get one like those lovely brown ones we saw at the dog show?" he pleaded.

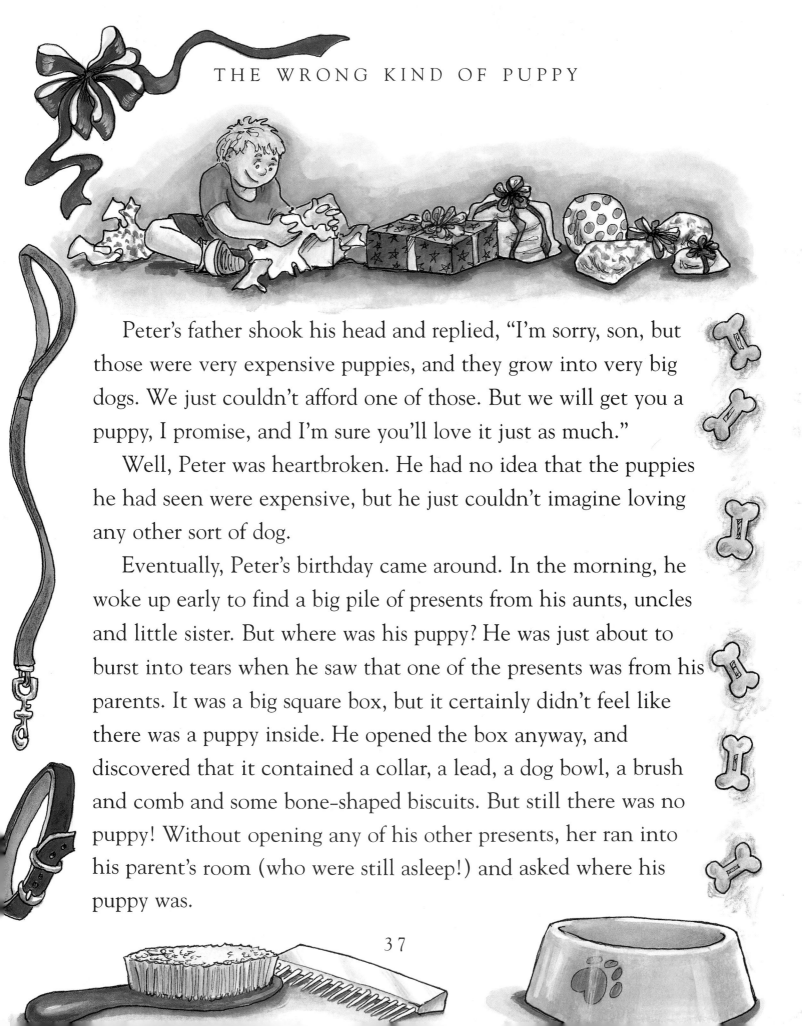

Peter's father shook his head and replied, "I'm sorry, son, but those were very expensive puppies, and they grow into very big dogs. We just couldn't afford one of those. But we will get you a puppy, I promise, and I'm sure you'll love it just as much."

Well, Peter was heartbroken. He had no idea that the puppies he had seen were expensive, but he just couldn't imagine loving any other sort of dog.

Eventually, Peter's birthday came around. In the morning, he woke up early to find a big pile of presents from his aunts, uncles and little sister. But where was his puppy? He was just about to burst into tears when he saw that one of the presents was from his parents. It was a big square box, but it certainly didn't feel like there was a puppy inside. He opened the box anyway, and discovered that it contained a collar, a lead, a dog bowl, a brush and comb and some bone-shaped biscuits. But still there was no puppy! Without opening any of his other presents, her ran into his parent's room (who were still asleep!) and asked where his puppy was.

"We have to go and collect it today," said his mother. "We've chosen you a lovely little puppy from the dogs' home that desperately needed a new family to look after it. We can go and get it as soon as we've had breakfast."

Peter was much too excited to eat any breakfast, of course, and spent the next half hour saying, "Can we go yet?" Eventually everyone was ready, and they all climbed into the car for the journey to the dogs' home. Peter sat in the back clutching the lead and hoping it wouldn't be too long before there was a puppy attached to the other end of it!

Soon they reached the dogs' home, and one of the kennel maids took them to where Peter's puppy was being kept. But when Peter first set eyes on the puppy, his heart sank. This wasn't anything like the sort of puppy he had wanted. Instead of being brown and fluffy and bouncy, this puppy was tiny and scraggy and timid. When it saw Peter and his family approach, it gave a little wag of its tail but then just stood in its cage whimpering.

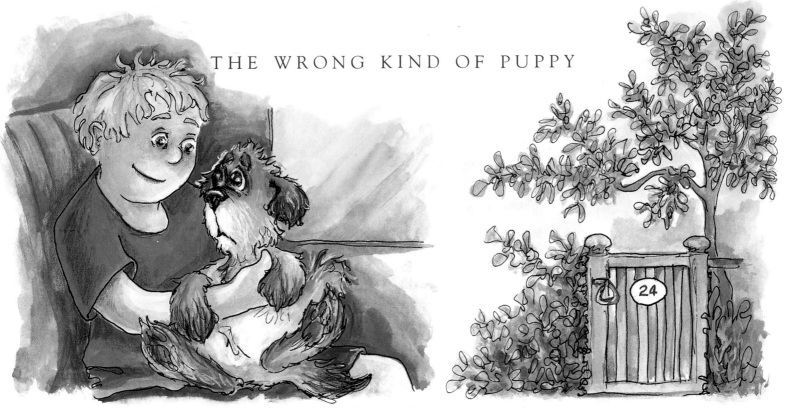

Now Peter had been taught by his parents that you must never be ungrateful for presents, even if they aren't exactly what you wanted. So although he was very disappointed, he reached out and stroked the puppy. The little scruffy puppy timidly approached Peter, licked his hand, and then ran off into the corner of the cage.

"He'll soon get used to you," said the kennel maid brightly. "Come on, Rags, time to go to your new home." And with that, she lifted the little puppy up and placed him in Peter's arms.

All the way home, the little puppy sat quietly in Peter's arms, occasionally trembling. Now and again he looked up at Peter with his big, soft eyes.

When they got Rags home, he was so frightened that he ran and hid under the curtains. Peter wondered how he was going to be able to play with such a timid friend.

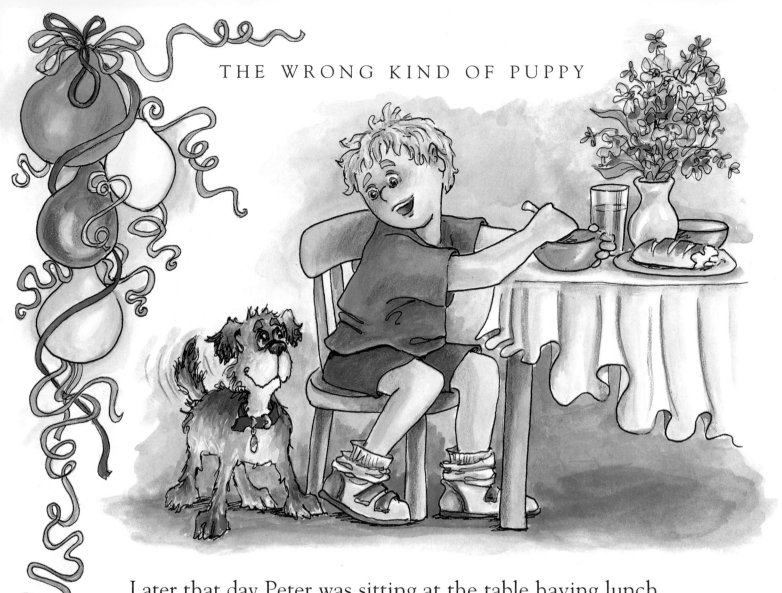

Later that day Peter was sitting at the table having lunch when he felt something cold and wet against his leg; it was Rags's nose. He peered down to see Rags looking up at him, his tail wagging backwards and forwards. "He's looking a bit happier now," said Peter's father. "It will only be a matter of time before he feels really at home here."

The next morning, Peter hurried downstairs as soon as he awoke to say good morning to Rags – because the truth was, although Rags wasn't quite like the puppy he had expected, he was really getting very fond of him.

Rags jumped out of his basket when he saw Peter, his tail wagging furiously. "He's quite a waggy dog after all," thought Peter. Then Rags picked up his ball and began to play with it. Every time Peter tried to take it, Rags scurried off with a wag of his tail, looking round to make sure that Peter was chasing him. He seemed to like playing after all!

As the days went by, Rags seemed to grow more and more playful. He would jump up and greet his family with a big lick and a wagging tail, he always wanted to go for walks and to play, and he was very quick to learn tricks.

Peter just couldn't believe how much Rags had changed from the timid little creature in the dogs' home to the happy, playful puppy he was now – all thanks to a little love and care.

But the most curious thing of all was the puppy's appearance. He had now grown a beautiful, fluffy coat and, if Peter wasn't very much mistaken, it was quite brown, too. And it matched the colour of his big, brown eyes.

Granny Casts a Spell

Susie was very fond of her Granny. Each day, when Susie got home from school, Granny was always there sitting by the fire knitting. Granny knitted so fast that sometimes it seemed as though the knitting needles sparked in the firelight.

"Do you know," Granny would say, "that I'm really a witch?" Susie always laughed when Granny said that because she didn't look at all like a witch. She had a smiling face and kind eyes and she never wore black. Not ever. When Granny wasn't looking, Susie would take a peek inside her wardrobe just in case she might find a broomstick or a witch's hat. But she never found so much as a book of spells.

"I don't believe you're a witch," said Susie.

"I am," replied Granny, "and I'll cast a spell one day. You'll know when that day comes, for my needles will start to knit by themselves." After that, Susie kept a careful watch over Granny's needles, but they always lay quite still in the basket of knitting.

One day, Susie was playing in her garden when she heard the sound of weeping. The sound seemed to be coming from under the old tree in the corner. She walked towards the tree and as she did so the crying noise got louder, but she could not see anyone there. Then she looked down at her feet and there – sitting on a mossy stone – was a tiny little man. He was neatly dressed in a yellow velvet waistcoat and knickerbockers. On his feet were beautiful, shiny, buckled shoes, and a three-cornered hat with a wren's feather in it trembled on his shaking head. When the little man saw Susie, he stopped crying and started to dab his eyes with a fine lace handkerchief.

"Whatever can the matter be?" asked Susie, crouching down.

"Oh dear, oh dear!" sobbed the little man, "I am the fairy princess's tailor and she has asked me to make her a lovely gown to wear to the May Ball tonight, but a wicked elf has played a trick on me and turned all my fine gossamer fabric into bats' wings. Now I shall never be able to make the princess's gown and she will be very angry with me." He started to cry again.

"Don't cry!" said Susie. "I'm sure I can help. My Granny's got a sewing basket full of odds and ends. I'll see if she's got anything nice for a party dress. I'm sure she won't mind sparing some – after all, you won't need much," she said. At that, the little man looked a bit more cheerful.

"Wait here," said Susie, "while I run indoors and see." She ran up the garden path and in through the back door.

"Granny, Granny!" she called. She ran into the sitting room expecting to find Granny knitting by the fire. But Granny had her eyes closed and she was whispering to herself. On her lap was her knitting – and the needles were moving all by themselves, so that the yarn danced up and down on the old lady's knees.

For a moment, Susie was too astounded to move. Then she thought, "I hope Granny's not casting a bad spell. I'd better make sure the little tailor is alright."

She ran back down the garden path and there under the tree sat the tailor, surrounded by a great pile of gorgeous gossamer, shining in the sunlight.

"I've never seen such fine material – ever!" he exclaimed. "But where did it come from? I just closed my eyes to dab them with my hanky and when I opened them again – there it was!"

"I don't know," said Susie, "but I think my Granny might have had something to do with it."

"Well, I'd never be able to thank her enough," said the tailor. "For now I shall be able to make the finest gown in the whole of fairyland. The princess will dance the night away in the prettiest dress there ever was." He paused and then went on, "I'm also indebted to you, for it was you who helped me in the first place. I would like it very much if you came to the May Ball, too."

"Why, thank you so much," Susie replied, "I should like that very much." She didn't want to hurt the tailor's feelings but she knew she couldn't go – she was far too big to go to a fairy ball!

"Well I must get on with the dress now," said the little man, reaching for a pair of fairy scissors. "See you tonight!" And with that he vanished.

Susie went indoors again. Granny was knitting by the fire as usual. Susie wondered if she had dreamed the whole thing. Everything seemed so normal. Really, how could she have imagined she'd seen a fairy tailor in the garden! And as for Granny casting a spell!

That night, Susie lay in bed and wondered if the fairies really were having a ball. How she longed to be there! Once she thought she heard a tapping at the window. Was that the fairy tailor she saw through the glass – or was she imagining it? In the middle of the night she awoke with a start. There was a click, clicking noise at the end of her bed.

"Granny is that you?" called Susie.

"Yes, dear," replied Granny. "I couldn't sleep, so I decided to do some knitting. All at once the needles started twitching, so I knew it was time to cast a spell. What is your wish, Susie?"

"I... I...," stammered Susie, "I want to go to the May Ball," she blurted.

"Then you shall, my dear," said Granny.

In an instant, Susie felt herself shrinking and when she looked down she saw she was wearing a beautiful gown and tiny satin slippers. Then she floated on gossamer wings out through the window and off to the Ball.

The next morning, Susie woke up in her bed. Had it all been a dream – the revelry, the fairy food, the frog band, the dance with the fairy prince? Then she saw something peeping out from under her pillow. And what do you think it was? It was a tiny, tiny shred of the finest gossamer fabric.

The Lost Lion

Once there was a lion cub called Lenny. He was a very tiny lion cub, but he was sure that he was the bravest lion in all of Africa. When his mother taught her cubs how to stalk prey, Lenny would stalk his own mother and pounce on her. When she showed them how to wash themselves, Lenny licked his sister's face instead so that she growled at him. When the mother lioness led her cubs down to the watering hole to drink, he jumped into the water and created a huge splash that soaked everyone.

The other lionesses were not amused. "You'd better watch that son of yours," they said to Lenny's mother, "or he'll get into really big trouble."

One day the mother lioness led her
cubs on their first big hunt. "Stay close to me,"
she said, "or you could get hurt."
She crawled off through the undergrowth with
her cubs following on behind, one after the other. Lenny was at
the back. The grass tickled his tummy and he wanted to laugh,
but he was trying hard to be obedient. So he crawled along,
making sure he kept the bobbing tail of the cub in front in sight.
On and on they crawled until Lenny was beginning to feel quite
weary.

"But a brave lion cub doesn't give up," he thought to himself.
And on he plodded.

At last the grass gave way to a clearing. Lenny looked up, and to
his dismay he saw that the tail he had been following was attached,
not to one of his brothers or sisters, but to a baby elephant!

49

Somewhere along the trail he had started following the wrong tail and now he was hopelessly lost. He wanted to cry out for his mother but then he remembered that he was the bravest lion in all of Africa. So what do you think he did? He went straight up to the mother elephant and growled his fiercest growl at her. "That'll frighten her!" thought Lenny. "She won't dare growl back!" And, of course, she didn't growl back. Instead she lifted her trunk and trumpeted so loudly at Lenny that he was blown off his feet and through the air and landed against the hard trunk of a tree.

Lenny got up and found that his knees were knocking. "Oh my," he thought, "that elephant has a very loud growl. But I'm still definitely the bravest lion in all of Africa." He set off across the plain. It was getting hot in the midday sun and soon Lenny began to feel sleepy. "I think I'll just take a nap in that tree," he thought, and started climbing up into the branches.

To his surprise, he found that the tree was already occupied by a large leopard. "I'll show him who's boss," thought Lenny, baring his tiny claws. The leopard raised his head to look at Lenny, and then bared his own huge, razor-sharp claws. He took a swipe at Lenny with his paw. Without even touching Lenny, the wind from the leopard's great paw swept Lenny out of the tree and he landed with a bump on the ground.

Lenny got up and found that his legs were trembling. "Oh my," he thought, "that leopard had big claws. But I'm still definitely the bravest lion in Africa." He set off again across the plain. After a while he began to feel quite hungry. "I wonder what I can find to eat," he thought. Just then he saw a spotted shape lying low in the grass. "That looks like a tasty meal," thought Lenny as he pounced on the spotted shape.

But the spotted shape was a cheetah! Quick as a flash, the cheetah sprang away and as he did so, his tail caught Lenny a blow that sent him spinning round and round in circles.

When Lenny stopped spinning, he got up and found that his whole body was shaking. "Oh my," he thought, "that cheetah is a fast runner." Then he added in rather a small voice, "But I'm still the bravest lion in Africa." He set off again across the plain. By now it was getting dark and Lenny was wishing he was at home with his mother and brothers and sisters. "I wonder if they've noticed I've gone," he thought sadly as a tear rolled down his furry cheek. He felt cold and tired and hungry as he crawled into the undergrowth to sleep.

Some time later Lenny was woken by a noise that was louder than anything he'd ever heard before – louder even than the elephant's trumpeting. It filled the night air and made the leaves on the trees shake. The noise was getting louder and louder and the animal that was making it was getting nearer and nearer. Lenny peeped out from his hiding place and saw a huge golden creature with big yellow eyes that shone in the dark like lamps. It had a great crown of shaggy golden fur all around its head and its red jaws were open wide revealing a set of very large white fangs. How it roared! Lenny was terrified and about to turn tail and run, when the animal stopped roaring and spoke to him. "Come here, Lenny," said the animal gently. "It's me, your father, and I'm going to take you home. Climb up on my back, little one."

So Lenny climbed up on his father's back and was carried all the way home. And when they got there his father told his mother and his brothers and sisters that Lenny had been a very brave lion after all.

The Sad Clown

Bongo the clown had a bit of a problem. Clowns were supposed to be happy, funny, jolly people, but Bongo was a very sad clown. Nothing at all seemed to make him laugh.

Whenever the circus came to town people from all around flocked to the big top hoping for an exciting day out. They thrilled to the daring performance of the high-wire act, as the acrobats leaped from one swinging trapeze to the next. They enjoyed the jugglers, who tossed bright, sparkling balls into the air while standing on one leg. And the crowd delighted in seeing the beautiful white horses parading around the circus ring with the bareback riders balancing on their backs. When the seals came on, there was always a big cheer from the crowd, for everyone loved them and could watch their clever antics for hours.

But the biggest favourite of the crowd, especially with all the children, was the clown. Dressed in his big baggy trousers he would enter the circus ring with his funny walk. Everyone laughed to see him. They laughed even more when they saw his big floppy hat with the revolving flower on it. Even his painted clown face made them laugh.

But when his act started, the crowd thought they would burst with laughter. First of all his bicycle fell apart as he tried to ride around the ring. Then he fell out of his motor car when the seat tipped up. By the time he had accidentally poured cold water down his trousers and fallen into the custard-filled swimming pool, the crowd were almost crying with laughter.

But beneath all the makeup, Bongo the sad clown wasn't smiling at all. In fact, he saw nothing funny at all in bicycles that fell apart as you used them, or cars that tipped you out as you went along, or having cold water poured down your trousers, or even ending up face first in a swimming pool full of custard. He simply hadn't got a sense of humour.

All the other performers in the circus decided they would try and cheer the sad clown up.

"I know," said the high-wire trapeze acrobat, "let's paint an even funnier face on him. That'll make him laugh."

So that's what they did, but Bongo still didn't laugh and was still just as sad.

"Let us perform some of our tricks, just for him," said the seals. So they sat on their stools and tossed their big coloured balls to each other, clapped their flippers together and made lots of honking sounds. But Bongo still didn't laugh. In fact, nothing that anyone tried made poor Bongo smile. He was still a very sad clown.

Then Percival the ring master spoke. "You know, I think I know what the problem is," he said. "There is nothing a clown likes better than playing tricks on other clowns. Perhaps if we had a second clown, that would cheer Bongo up."

So right away they hired another clown, called Piffle.

The circus arrived in the next town and soon it was time for Bongo and Piffle's act. Piffle started riding around on his bike while Bongo pretended to wash the car by throwing a bucket of water over it. Instead of the water landing on the car, of course, it went all over Piffle, who just happened to be cycling past at that moment. A little smile flickered across Bongo's face at the sight of the soaking wet Piffle.

Next, Bongo and Piffle pretended to be cooking, and Bongo tripped while carrying two huge custard pies. Both landed right in Piffle's face. Bongo let out a huge chuckle of laughter when he saw Piffle's custard-covered face.

THE SAD CLOWN

At the end of their act, the clowns were pretending to be decorators, painting up a ladder. Of course, you've guessed it. The ladders fell down and all the pots of paint landed on the two clowns. Bongo looked across at Piffle, who had a big paint pot stuck on his head, with paint dripping down his body. Bongo threw back his head and roared with laughter. Piffle thought Bongo looked just as funny with paint all over his body, too. And as for the crowd – well, they thought two clowns were even funnier than one and they clapped and cheered and filled the big top with laughter. After that Bongo was never a sad clown again.

The Dog With No Voice

There once lived a prince whose words were pure poetry. He amused the court with his witty, rhyming verse, yet his kind and thoughtful words made him popular with all. It was said he could even charm the birds from the trees.

One day, he was walking in the forest when he came upon an old lady with a huge bundle on her back. "Let me help," said the prince. He took the load and walked along beside the woman. They chatted away and before long they had reached the old lady's door.

Now the old lady – who was really a witch – had been listening intently to the prince's words. "What a fine voice he has!" she thought to herself. "I would like my own son to speak like that. Then maybe he could find himself a wealthy wife and we'd be rich for ever more!"

"You must be thirsty," she said to the prince. "Let me give you something to quench your thirst to repay you for your kindness." The prince gratefully accepted, and was given a delicious drink which he drained to the last drop. He was about to thank the witch when he began to feel very peculiar. He found he was getting smaller and smaller. He looked down at his feet and saw two hairy paws. Then he turned round and saw to his horror that he had grown a shaggy tail! He tried to shout at the witch but all that came out of his mouth was a loud bark!

The witch hugged herself for joy. "My spell worked!" she cackled. "Come here my son!" she called.

There appeared at the door a rough-looking young man. "What's going on, my dearest mother?" he said in a voice that sounded familiar to the prince. Then he looked down and exclaimed, "Where did you find this poor little dog?"

Now the prince understood what had happened. "The old lady has turned me into a humble hound and given my voice to her son. Whatever am I to do?" he thought miserably. "I can't return to the palace. They'll never let a stray dog in." He turned with his tail between his legs and trotted off forlornly into the forest.

The witch and her son were delighted with his new voice. She made him scrub himself clean from top to toe and dressed him in the prince's clothes. "Now go," she said, "and don't return until you've found a rich girl to marry!"

The young man set off, eager to try out his new voice. Soon he was feeling very pleased with himself as he talked to passers-by. "What a very polite young man!" and "What a wonderful way with words," folk cried. "He could charm the birds out of the trees," other people said.

The witch's son travelled far and wide until at last he came to a castle where he spied a fair princess sitting on her balcony. He called to her and straight away she arose and looked down into the garden, enraptured by the sound of his beautiful voice. She was enchanted by his fine words and guessed they must belong to a prince. Soon the princess and the witch's son were chatting away merrily, and to his delight when he asked her to marry him she readily agreed. "For one with so beautiful a voice," she thought to herself, "must indeed be a fine young man."

Meanwhile, the poor dog-prince wandered in the forest, surviving as best he could by foraging for roots and fruits in the undergrowth. Feeling truly miserable, he stopped to drink from a stream. As he dipped his long dog's tongue in the cool water, he caught sight of someone sitting on a bridge. It was a pixie, fishing with a tiny net.

"Cheer up!" said the little fellow, "I saw everything that happened and I think I know how we can get your voice back. Follow me!" And with that he was off, dancing away through the forest with the dog-prince trotting along behind. They seemed to go on forever, and the dog-prince was feeling very hot, and the pads of his paws were quite sore, by the time they reached the castle. He could see the witch's son in the garden calling to the princess on the balcony. The dog-prince's eyes filled with tears, for she was quite the loveliest girl he had ever seen and he wished he could marry her himself.

"We will be married today," the witch's son was saying in the prince's voice, "I will await you by the church, my fairest one." Seizing his fishing net, the pixie leaped high in the air. As the words 'my fairest one' floated up to the balcony, he caught them in the net and gave them back to the dog-prince.

As soon as he had swallowed the words, the dog-prince could speak again. "Thank you, little pixie," he cried, "but what can I do? Now I am a dog with a prince's voice. The princess will never marry me."

"If you want to break the witch's spell, you must go to the church – fast!" said the pixie. And with those words he disappeared.

Straight away, the dog-prince ran to the church door. There was the princess looking most perplexed, for standing beside her was the witch's son – with not a word in his head. "I don't understand," she cried, "I thought I was to marry a silver–tongued young man, but now I find he is a dumb ragamuffin!"

"I can explain," exclaimed the dog-prince.

The princess spun around. "Who can explain?" she asked, for all she could see was a dog in front of her. "What a handsome dog!" she cried, bending down and kissing him on the nose. To her astonishment, the dog's hairy paws and shaggy tail immediately disappeared and there stood the prince. "But you're... but he..." she stammered looking from the prince to the witch's son.

Well, the prince explained everything that had happened, and after that he and the princess were married with great rejoicing. And as for the witch's son? He wasn't a bad young man, really, so the prince taught him to speak again – with a beautiful voice – and he married the princess's younger sister.

The Chocolate Soldier

In the window of Mrs Brown's sweet shop there stood a chocolate soldier. He had chocolate ears, chocolate eyebrows and a curly chocolate moustache of which he was particularly proud. But best of all he loved his shiny foil uniform with its braid on the shoulders and cuffs, and smart red stripes down each leg. All day long the chocolate soldier stood to attention on a shelf in the window, staring straight ahead out into the street. Standing next to him on the shelf were more chocolate soldiers, and beyond them he could see some sugar mice and a twist of liquorice bootlaces.

It was summer time and the sun shone through the window of the sweet shop. At first the chocolate soldier felt pleasantly warm; then he started to feel uncomfortably hot. Next he began to feel most peculiar indeed. His chocolate moustache was wilting and his arms were dripping. Soon he was completely melted and before he knew it, he had slipped out through a hole in his silver foil shoe and was pouring off the shelf and out into the street.

Down the street he poured.

"Stop! Help!" he shouted, but nobody heard his cries. Now he could hear the sound of gushing water and, to his horror, he could see he was heading for a stream at the bottom of the street.

"Help me! I can't swim! I'm going to drown!" the chocolate soldier cried as he plunged into the cold, running water. But now something very strange was happening. He found he could swim quite easily. He looked round and saw that he had a chocolate tail covered in scales. He looked down at his arms, but there was a pair of fins instead. The cold water had hardened him into the shape of a chocolate fish!

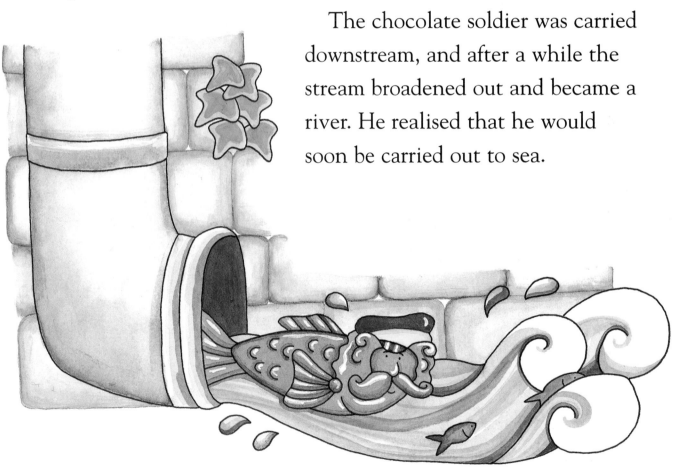

The chocolate soldier was carried downstream, and after a while the stream broadened out and became a river. He realised that he would soon be carried out to sea.

"Whatever shall I do?" wondered the chocolate soldier. "I'm sure to get eaten by a bigger fish or maybe even a shark!" He tried to turn around and swim against the river's flow but it was no good. The current swept him away down river again.

Soon he could see the waves on the shore. He smelt the sea air and tasted the salt in the water. Now he found himself bobbing up and down on the sea. He could see a boat not far away and then all of a sudden he felt a net closing around him. He struggled to get out, but the net only tightened and soon he felt himself being hauled out of the water and landed with a "thwack!" on the deck among a pile of fish. The smell was awful, and the chocolate soldier was quite relieved when he felt the boat being rowed towards the shore.

"I'll hop over the side as soon as we land and run away," he thought, quite forgetting that he had no legs but only a fish's tail.

But there was no chance of escape. As soon as the boat reached the shore, he and all the other fish were flung into buckets and lifted into a van. The van stopped outside a shop and a man carried the buckets inside, where it smelt of fried fish, chips and vinegar. The chocolate soldier found himself being lifted up with a lot of other fish in a huge metal basket. He looked down and saw a terrible sight below. They were heading for a vat of boiling oil! At that very moment he felt very peculiar once again. His scales melted, his tail drooped and he felt himself slide through the holes in the basket and into the pocket of a man's overalls.

The chocolate soldier lay in the corner of the pocket, while the man worked all day in the shop. Then the man headed for home, with the chocolate soldier bouncing up and down in the overall pocket as the man walked along. Soon they arrived at the man's house. He reached into his pocket.

"Look what I've found," he said to his small son. "A coin. Here, you can have it – but don't spend it all at once!" he said, chuckling to himself. The chocolate soldier felt himself being passed from one hand to another.

"So now I've hardened into the shape of a chocolate coin," he thought. "And I'm going to be eaten by the boy!" But to his surprise he found himself being slipped into the boy's pocket.

The chocolate soldier felt himself bouncing up and down in the child's pocket as he ran up the street and into a shop. The chocolate soldier peeped out and to his astonishment saw that he was back in Mrs Brown's sweet shop. Then he realised what was happening. The boy believed he was a real coin and was going to try and spend him! The boy stood in the queue at the counter.

The chocolate soldier called out to his soldier friends in the window, "Pssst! It's me! Help me get out of here!" One of the soldiers looked down, but all he could see was a chocolate coin sticking out of the boy's pocket. Then he recognised the voice.

"I'm a chocolate soldier like you, but I've been turned into a coin. Help!" cried the chocolate soldier.

"Leave it to me," replied the soldier on the shelf. "Don't worry, we'll have you out of there in a jiffy!"

The word was passed along and, quick as a flash, one of the sugar mice chewed off a length of liquorice bootlace. Then the soldier lowered the lace into the boy's pocket, where it stuck to the chocolate coin. Carefully the soldiers hauled the coin up on to the shelf. The chocolate soldier was delighted to find his foil uniform was still there on the shelf, just where it had been before. All the effort of getting on to the shelf had made him quite warm, and he found he could slip quite easily back through the hole in the shoe and into his uniform again.

"I'd like a chocolate soldier," said the boy to Mrs Brown. But when he reached in his pocket the coin had gone.

"Never mind," said kind Mrs Brown, "I'll let you have one anyway." She reached into the window and took down a soldier from the end of the row and gave it to the boy. And as for our chocolate soldier? In the cool of the night he turned back into a smart-looking soldier again.

No Hunting!

Mr Rabbit opened his eyes and gave a big yawn. He thought it seemed like the perfect day for going outside and nibbling some of the farmer's lettuces. And after that he thought he would go and see how well the farmer's carrots were growing, and maybe have a little nibble of those as well. He popped his head out of his burrow and looked this way and that, in case he saw any danger. Then he pricked up his ears and turned this way and that, in case he heard any danger. Finally, he sniffed the air this way and that, in case he smelled any danger. It seemed safe, so he hopped out of his burrow.

No sooner had he gone a couple of steps when "ZING" – a bullet whizzed past his head. Mr Rabbit jumped back into his burrow as fast as he could go, shaking with fright.

"Goodness, it's the rabbit hunting season," he gasped. He gathered his family of young rabbits around him and spoke to them. "Now children, listen very carefully," he said. "The rabbit hunting season has begun, so you must all stay safely inside the burrow until it's over. I will go out at night and forage for food for us all."

His children looked at him in dismay. "But it's lovely and sunny outside," they cried all together. "We'll be very careful."

But Mr Rabbit was having none of it. He insisted that they all stay under ground until the rabbit season was over.

For a few days, the young rabbits amused themselves as best they could by playing chase and hide and seek. But they were becoming very bored. Finally, they decided that they were going to do something to stop the rabbit hunting themselves.

First Tom, the eldest of Mr Rabbit's children, decided he would try and stop the hunters. So when it was dark, he crept out of the burrow and made his way towards the hunters' hut.

Although it was night and he was sure the hunters would be asleep, he was still very scared. Soon he came to the hut. It was standing in a clearing in the woods. It was dark inside the hut and he hoped the hunters were asleep. "If I can dig some big holes," he thought, "maybe they will fall into them in the morning and won't be able to get out until the hunting season is over."

So he dug and he dug like he had never dug before. Soon there were holes everywhere, right outside the door to the hunters' hut. Feeling very pleased with himself, but also very tired, Tom made his way back to the burrow just before it was light.

When the hunters awoke, they went straight out without falling down a single hole! Poor Tom, he had dug lots of holes alright, but the hunters' hut had two doors, and the hunters had simply gone out of the other one!

Then Jenny, the second oldest of Mr Rabbit's children, decided that she would try and stop the hunters. So when it was dark, she crept out of the burrow and made her way towards the hunters' hut. When she got there, she noticed that the window was open and so she decided to go inside. She, too, was very scared, but she thought about having to spend all those days in the burrow until the hunting season was over and that gave her the courage to carry on.

Inside the hut, she could see the hunters sleeping in their beds. She looked around, wondering what she could do to stop them hunting. Then suddenly she saw the hunters' clothes lying on a chair. Quick as a flash, she hopped up to them and started nibbling at them. In no time at all, the clothes were in shreds. "That'll stop them," thought Jenny. "They can't hunt without their clothes on!" Satisfied with her night's work, Jenny made her way back to the burrow just as dawn was breaking.

When the hunters awoke, they got straight up and went out hunting! Poor Jenny, she had chewed some clothes alright, but she had only chewed some spare clothes! The hunters had gone to bed wearing their other clothes in order to be out quickly in the morning.

Finally, Penelope, the youngest of Mr Rabbit's children, said she would try and stop the hunters.

"Don't be silly," said Tom to his sister. "You are far too young to be going out at night."

"And anyway," said Jenny, "what could you possibly think of doing to stop the hunters?"

"I'll think of something," said Penelope, who was really quite a clever little rabbit.

So that night, she crept out of the burrow and made her way to the hunters' hut. The window was open, just as before, and so Penelope hopped inside. She looked on the floor, she looked in the cupboards, and she looked under the beds, but she couldn't think of anything to stop the hunters.

Then she looked up and suddenly had an idea. For there on the table was a calendar, showing that very day's date. Penelope hopped on to the table and started to turn the pages. Finally she came to a page on the calendar that read: "RABBIT HUNTING SEASON ENDS TODAY". Satisfied with her work, Penelope hopped out of the hunters' hut and back home to her burrow.

In the morning, the hunters woke up, rubbed their eyes and got out of their beds. One of them glanced at the calendar. "Oh no!" he suddenly exclaimed. "Look at the date! The rabbit hunting season is over."

With that, the hunters (who were too silly to realise that someone else must have turned over the pages of the calendar) packed their belongings and went home. All was peace and quiet once more and the rabbits could hop about in the open air in safety.

The Mirror of Dreams

The house on the corner of Nightingale Avenue was tall and very handsome, and was by far the largest in the neighbourhood. From the street you could see four floors of beautifully decorated rooms, and if you peeped over the railings you could see the basement below. If you were lucky enough to be asked into the house, and passed through the beautiful hallways into the playroom, you might meet the owner's daughter, Cordelia. Sometimes Cordelia would be sitting in her silk pyjamas playing on her grand piano, and sometimes she would be dressed in the finest velvet gowns playing with her lovely dolls.

If you went down the stairs and into the basement, you might come across Polly. Polly's mother was a chambermaid in the house, and worked hard all day long to make the house sparkling clean. Sometimes Polly helped her to polish the ornaments and dust the furniture, but more often Polly sat on her own in her small bedroom drawing pictures with some crayons on a drawing pad she had been given for her birthday. When Polly was helping to polish the furniture she would look longingly at all of

Cordelia's fine clothes and toys, and when she sat alone in her room she would draw pictures of all the beautiful things she would like to own if only she could afford them.

One day, a large parcel was delivered to the house and taken upstairs to Cordelia's bedroom. A little while later, Cordelia's maid carried a pretty, ornate mirror down from her room and put it with the rubbish waiting for collection outside the house. Polly asked the maid why the mirror was to be thrown away, and the maid explained that Cordelia had been given a new mirror in which to brush her long, silky locks, and that she didn't need it any more. The maid then asked if Polly would like the old mirror, and of course Polly accepted with pleasure – it was the most beautiful thing she had ever owned.

Polly carried the mirror back to her room and polished it lovingly. As she polished the glass a strange thing started to happen. The glass went misty, and then cleared as her own reflection stared back at her once more. But the reflection that stared back was not dressed in rags and worn old clothes as Polly was, but in a rich gown of the most beautiful cream satin, with pink bows and apricot lace.

Polly was entranced. She looked almost as beautiful as Cordelia! Her hair gleamed and her fingers were white and magnificent. As she looked further into the mirror, she saw herself dancing at a ball, and then sitting down to eat the finest food she had ever seen – hams and roasted meats, and cakes of strawberries and cream!

And then the mirror spoke to her. "I am the Mirror of Dreams," the cool, clear voice said. "Whatever your heart desires most will be reflected in my shiny surface."

Polly was astounded, but so happy. She didn't care that it was only a day dream, for when she saw her reflection in the beautiful clothes, she felt as if she were truly there dancing and eating the fine foods – she could almost taste the fruit and cream in her mouth!

From that day on, Polly sat in her room every day, and dreamed and dreamed and dreamed. She had never felt so happy before, and could not wait to wake up each morning to visit her imaginary world. She certainly didn't understand how Cordelia could have thrown away such a magical wonder, and thought that she could not have known of its enchanting secret. She supposed also that Cordelia could have had no use for such a mirror, for whatever Cordelia wanted in real life she received, and would have no need to dream. But Polly was to find out that this was very far from true!

Weeks passed, and every day Polly sat and dreamed of ermine cloaks, of diamonds and pearls, of parties and picnics and carnivals. Eventually, she had dreamed every dream she had ever wanted. And Polly began to realise that it no longer made her as happy as it once had, and she began to grow weary of her Mirror of Dreams. She sat in front of the mirror less and less, and eventually when she did visit the mirror she could not think of a single thing that would make her happy. Even the dreams she had in which her mother wore fine silk clothes and didn't have to scrub and clean for their living could no longer make her happy.

She preferred her real mother, who came to kiss her good night and read her stories no matter how tired and overworked she was. Eventually she stopped looking in the mirror altogether, and finally decided to throw the mirror away – it had only made her more unhappy.

As the long winter turned into spring she acted upon her decision, and took down the mirror to throw away with the rubbish. But as she looked into the glass, it misted over in its familiar way and she saw herself in the mirror as she looked in real life, but in it she was playing with other children like herself, and reading stories with them and sharing toys. She felt gloriously happy, and knew in that instant that all she wanted was a very good friend. She realised in that moment, too, that perhaps Cordelia really had known the mirror's secret, but that she also had become more unhappy as the dreams faded and reality forced itself upon her. She wondered aloud what it was that Cordelia had dreamed of, and for the second and last time the mirror spoke in its cool, clear voice.

"The Mirror of Dreams showed Cordelia her heart's desire, and her heart desires a true friend and companion – someone who is not jealous of her wealth, but a friend who will share her hopes and dreams, and with whom she can have parties, games and picnics."

Polly put the mirror down and thought with amazement that she could be that friend, if Cordelia would be friends with someone poor but honest and true. Polly left the mirror with the household rubbish and was about to make the descent back to the basement, when she saw Cordelia standing in the garden at the back of the house. Cordelia had seen her discard the mirror, and shyly walked up to Polly. Polly overcame her shyness also and went to meet Cordelia, and then she told her they shared the same dream.

Cordelia and Polly became the best of friends from that day on. They shared everything they had, no matter how much or little. They talked and laughed together all day long, and they played long into the evening. They didn't have to dream any more, for they had both got their true heart's desire.

The Missing Scarf

Kanga was very proud of her stripy knitted scarf. She had made it herself and she had also made a smaller matching one for her son, Joey. Kanga used to hop through the bush with her scarf streaming out behind her, while Joey's could just be seen poking out of the top of her pouch. Now Joey was older, he was too big for Kanga's pouch, but he still wore his scarf as he hopped along beside his mother.

Then one day Kanga woke up to find that her beautiful scarf was missing. She searched high and low but it was nowhere to be found. Eventually she decided that she would have to go out into the bush to look for it.

"Stay here," she said to Joey. "I'll try not to be long. I'm sure to find my scarf soon." Kanga hopped off into the bush and started to search among the roots of trees and under stones.

She had gone quite a long way when, looking up into the branches of a eucalyptus tree, she spotted Koala. Now Koala was usually to be found asleep, but this time she was busy preparing a meal of eucalyptus leaves for her children. Kanga looked up at Koala and then her jaw dropped. For Koala was quite clearly wearing Kanga's scarf around her tummy. Then, to Kanga's horror, she saw Koala use the end of the scarf to wipe the teacups! "Koala," Kanga called. "Whatever do you think you're doing?"

Koala stopped cleaning the teacups and looked down through the branches of the eucalyptus tree at Kanga. "I'm wiping my teacups with my apron," she replied sleepily, "and I'll thank you not to interfere!" And with that, she yawned and moved several branches further up the tree.

Poor Kanga felt very embarrassed. How could she have mistaken Koala's striped apron for her own scarf? She hopped away and carried on further into the bush. After a while she could hear Kookaburra's familiar laughing call nearby. "I know," thought Kanga, "I'll ask her if she's seen my scarf. She'd be able to spot it easily from up in the sky." She followed the sound of Kookaburra's call until she came to the tree where she lived. She looked up and, sure enough, there was Kookaburra flying towards the tree. Kanga was about to call up when her jaw dropped again. For Kookaburra was quite clearly carrying Kanga's scarf in her beak. "Kookaburra," Kanga called. "Whatever do you think you're doing?"

"I'm lining my nest," mumbled Kookaburra through a beakful of stripy feathers. "And I'll thank you not to interfere," she added more distinctly, for she had now reached the nest and was arranging the feathers carefully in place.

86

Poor Kanga felt even more embarrassed. How could she have mistaken the feathers for her own scarf? She hopped away and carried on further into the bush. After a while she reached a wide open plain and there she saw Emu running past with his baby chicks on his back. As he rushed past, Kanga's jaw dropped yet again. For Emu quite clearly had Kanga's scarf tucked in among his chicks. "Emu," called Kanga. "Whatever do you think you're doing?"

"I'm taking my chicks to safety," said Emu, glancing up at the sky as he sped away. "And you'd be wise to do the same," he added. Then Kanga realised that what she had thought was her rolled-up scarf were just the striped chicks on Emu's back.

Poor Kanga felt even more embarrassed. How could she have made such a mistake? Then she felt a few spots of rain on her nose and, looking up, saw a huge black cloud overhead. There was no time to lose – she must find shelter.

She made a dash for some trees at the edge of the plain and soon found herself by a stream. She wandered along beside the stream feeling cold, wet, tired and miserable. Finally, she lay down in the wet grass beside the stream and tried to get to sleep. She shivered with cold and wondered how Joey was and whether he was behaving himself. She so hoped he hadn't got into mischief.

Just then there was a tap on her shoulder and there stood Platypus. "I could hear you in my burrow over there," she said pointing towards a hole beside the stream just above the water. "I thought you might like this to keep you warm," she added.

"My scarf!" exclaimed Kanga.

"Oh, is that what it is? I'm ever so sorry," said Platypus. "I've been using it as a blanket for my babies. It's rather cold and damp in my burrow, you know," she added, rather forlornly.

"Where did you find it?" asked Kanga.

"It was stuck on some thorns and I know I shouldn't have taken it, but I just thought it would be so nice for keeping my young ones warm," blurted Platypus, and she started to sob.

"There now," said Kanga, "don't cry. You can keep the scarf. You need it more than me."

Platypus stopped crying and looked overjoyed. "Thank you," she said.

"No, thank you," said Kanga. "I've learned a lesson, which is not to get upset over a scarf, for I've ended up falling out with my friends."

Kanga made her way back home, but it took a long time because she apologised to all her friends on the way. When she explained what had happened Emu, Kookaburra and Koala all forgave her, and by the time she reached home she was feeling much better. Joey was there to greet her. "What have you been up to while I was away?" she asked.

"I made you this," he said. He handed her a scarf. It was a very funny-looking scarf, made out of twigs, grass and feathers, but Kanga loved it very much.

"This is much more special than my old scarf," she said. And she gave Joey an extra big hug.

Little Tim and His Brother Sam

Little Tim was a very lucky boy. He had a lovely home, with the nicest parents you could hope for. He had a big garden, with a swing and a football net in it. And growing in the garden were lots of trees that you could climb and have adventures in. Little Tim even had a nice school, which he enjoyed going to every day and where he had lots of friends. In fact, almost everything in Tim's life was nice. Everything that is apart from one thing – Tim's brother Sam.

Sam was a very naughty boy. Worse still, whenever he got into mischief – which he did almost all of the time – he managed to make it look as though someone else was to blame. And that someone was usually poor Tim!

Once Sam thought that he would put salt in the sugar bowl instead of sugar. That afternoon, Sam and Tim's parents had some friends round for tea. All the guests put salt in their cups of tea, of course, thinking it was sugar. Well, being very polite they didn't like to say anything, even though their cups of tea tasted very strange indeed! When Sam and Tim's parents tasted their tea, however, they guessed immediately that someone had been playing a trick. They had to apologise to their guests and make them all fresh cups of tea. And who got the blame? Little Tim did, because Sam had sprinkled salt on Tim's bedroom floor so that their mother would think that Tim was the culprit.

Another time, Sam and Tim were playing football in the garden when Sam accidentally kicked the ball against a window and broke it. Sam immediately ran away and hid, so that when their father came out to investigate, only Tim was to be seen. So poor little Tim got the blame again.

Then there was the time when Sam and Tim's Aunt Jessica came to stay. She was a very nice lady, but she hated anything creepy-crawly, and as far as she was concerned that included frogs. So what did Sam do? Why, he went down to the garden pond and got a big, green frog to put in Aunt Jessica's handbag When Aunt Jessica opened her handbag to get her glasses out, there staring out of the bag at her were two froggy eyes.

"Croak!" said the frog.

"Eeek!" yelled Aunt Jessica and almost jumped out of her skin.

"I told Tim not to do it," said Sam.

Tim opened his mouth and was just about to protest his innocence when his mother said, "Tim, go to your room immediately and don't come out until you are told."

Poor Tim went to his room and had to stay there until after supper. Sam thought it was very funny.

The next day, Sam decided that he would play another prank and blame it on Tim. He went to the garden shed and, one by one, took out all the garden tools. When he thought no-one was watching, he hid them all in Tim's bedroom cupboard. In went the spade, the fork, the watering can, the trowel – in fact, everything except the lawnmower. And the only reason that the lawnmower didn't go in was because it was too heavy to carry!

But this time, Sam's little prank was about to come unstuck, for Aunt Jessica had seen him creeping up the stairs to Tim's bedroom with the garden tools. She guessed immediately what Sam was up to, and who was likely to get the blame. When Sam wasn't about, she spoke to Tim. The two of them whispered to each other for a few seconds and then smiled triumphantly.

Later that day, Sam and Tim's father went to the garden shed to do some gardening. Imagine his surprise when all he saw were some old flower pots and the lawnmower. He searched high and low for the garden tools. He looked behind the compost heap, under the garden steps, behind the sand pit and in the garage. But they weren't anywhere to be seen.

Then he started searching in the house. He looked in the kitchen cupboard, and was just looking under the stairs when something at the top of the stairs caught his eye. The handle from the garden spade was sticking out of the door to Sam's bedroom. Looking rather puzzled, he went upstairs and walked into Sam's bedroom. There, nestling neatly in the cupboard, were the rest of the tools.

"Sam, come up here immediately," called his father.

Sam, not realising anything was amiss, came sauntering upstairs. Suddenly he saw all the garden tools that he had carefully hidden in Tim's cupboard now sitting in *his* cupboard. He was speechless.

"Right," said his father, "before you go out to play, you can take all the tools back down to the garden shed. Then you can cut the grass. Then you can dig over the flower beds, and then you can do the weeding."

Well, it took Sam hours to do all the gardening. Tim and Aunt Jessica watched from the window and clutched their sides with laughter. Sam never did find out how all the garden tools found their way into his bedroom, but I think you've guessed, haven't you?